EXITING THE PARTY (SEVEN STAGES)

Exiting the Party
(Seven Stages)

ISBN: 978-1-64826-841-0

Edited by Molly Gilley
Content editors: Molly Gilley
Cover Design: Jack Kinyon
Cover Photo: Akira Hojo

DEDICATION

I dedicate this book to the folks in my friend circle who have entertained me over the years as we attended many gatherings. They provided comic relief to me as I watched the tug-of-war between husband and wife as one was ready to leave while the other was just hitting their stride.

I especially would like to call out Jeff who made STAYING an art. It tickled me to no end to see the variety of ways that kept him from leaving. Susan, you and I are cut from the same cloth.

Mostly, to my wife and children who have had to live with my rigid personality these many years. I love you all. Blair, Kaleigh, Zoë and Gabriel, you've all taught me so much. Thank you. I know I wasn't the most fun of the parents, but I managed to keep you all out of jail and I guess that's what counts the most, right?

Jacqueline, you have transformed my life. When I penned my very first ISO ad in 1994, I was looking for a spontaneous woman. You certainly did not disappoint me in that area. I cannot express in words the joy you have brought to my life. Thank you for tolerating me and my dumb jokes. There is a special place for you in heaven.

Contents

ACKNOWLEDGEMENTS

A special thank you to Molly Gilley for editing this book. Molly gets me more than anybody. She makes me laugh.

Thank you, Zoë for your brief editing of the earlier edition of this book. I knew that English degree would pay itself off one day.

Thank you, Amy Hunter for your early read on the book and constructive feedback which helped me push this over the finish line.

Thank you, Douglas Bond for sitting with me at the pub in Cambridge, England, sharing a beer and asking the right question. "Who is my audience". And for your perfect punting advice. Because of you, I did not end up in the canal when the pole got stuck. WHEW!

Finally, thank you Jacqueline for your encouragement over the years, your impromptu edits and for making me laugh. This would have been so much easier to write if I had your grasp of grammar.

FORWARD

Are you a Leaver or a Stayer? Do you naturally linger at the conclusion of a social event or are you meticulously planning your escape prior to arrival?

Bill Yaich is my "same boat" friend. We are both planning that exit but we live with and love the beautiful Stayers as well.

Bill navigates this sometimes touchy terrain with wisdom, psychology and his special brand of wry wit. You will find yourself nodding your head in agreement no matter your side of the quandary.

Worth the read for the sheer grins along the way.

Molly Gilley
http://mgstudioart.com/

The book you hold in your hands is the culmination of many years of people-watching. Fortunately (if you ask me), or unfortunately (if you ask my wife), I have given him much fodder for the contents of this book.

Bill has been a good friend of mine for many years and besides his keen people observation skills, he is an intelligent interpreter of our pre-disposed ways of thinking and acting. He has the ability to succinctly wrap everything up into a neat little ball and deliver his conclusions with humorous sarcasm which causes many of us sit in wonder of his trenchant wit. As a professional "Stayer" I would love for Bill to attempt climbing inside the mind of a Stayer in a sequel to this first publication. He truly would stand amazed at the vastness of the relational possibilities a Stayer imagines. If he indeed would go there, he might choose to never come back.

I hope you enjoy this little edition and if you can temporarily put aside your preference for one type of Leaver over another, come to see how there really is great humor to be found in all of our diversities and idiosyncrasies.

Jeff Whitted
http://aslaninteriors.com/

PREFACE

For one to do even two minutes of research, one will find many articles or books that basically state the differences between men and women.

REALLY? Did we really need a study to tell us men and women are different? Any three-year-old could have saved the authors of these studies millions of dollars and thousands of hours of research. Just watch the way they play. It doesn't take a rocket scientist to see the chaos that follows the boys and the dainty house playing of girls.

Maybe I should seek grant money to research whether the temperature is different between Alaska and Hawaii.

Now I generalize a bit in my previous statement, but I think you get the point.

Move ahead 30 years or so and follow those same boys and girls who are now men and women. One only needs to view the habits of these men and women as they prepare to leave any gathering to see the differences.

Over the years, I've developed several theories. For instance, I figured out that women seem to belong to the same lodge. They gather at many various locations and seem to do all their voting for new officers in the lady's rooms at concerts or ball games or any large event which has them at one large meeting location at the same time. But that's a theory to be vetted in greater detail in another book.

My current theory is there are seven stages people go through to eventually leave any gathering. I'm sure we could even break it out into sub-stages. Additionally, there seems to be three stages of arriving as well. You can tell the couples who have successfully conquered the three stages of arriving. They are usually the first couples that actually manage to arrive on time. This doesn't necessarily mean both are champions at arriving. You only need one alpha member to force the other into arriving on time.

But once there, the games begin for entering and exiting the seven stages of leaving. In the chapters to follow I will outline these seven stages. See if you can see yourself or your significant other in any of these stages.

Maybe some time in the near future I'll tie some personality profile information to the stages which should help you better understand each other's point of view and to alleviate some of the angst felt by the one who would REALLY like to leave and the angst felt by the one who would REALLY, REALLY like to stay.

Thus, the problem is defined. Angst is felt by all in one form or another. One is jockeying for position by the front door while the other avoids eye contact with the significant other at all cost. One has the look of frustration written all over their face while the other obliviously laughs in the corner with the other Stayers.

I started this chapter talking about the differences between men and women. Early on, as I was developing my thoughts about this, I made the mistake of generalizing that men were most interested in leaving quickly and women were the part of the pair who wanted to linger. I found this not to be a correct assumption. But much like the studies which point out that men and women are different, so there are differences between the person who is looking for the quick exit and the person who is content to stay and relate. Leavers and Stayers are gender neutral. But the traits associated with both are obvious and requires little research to notice the differences between the two.

(NOTE: From this point forward, I will use the gender-neutral terms, Leaver and Stayer.)

As I've been bantering these theories around in my head over the years, I thought it prudent to see what the experts say about leaving.

At the end of each chapter you will find a section called "WHAT THE EXPERTS SAY". I added this section to give you a sense of how others perceive this never-ending struggle to stay or leave.

It's not surprising to me, for the most part, the experts address the introverts in their literature. If you're wondering why that is, it's probably because you haven't quite yet grasped the "nuanced" differences between the Introverts and Extroverts.

One last addition to each chapter will be a journal section. You can use this to journal the thoughts you have while waiting for your significant other to leave. Be creative. Before you know it, you may have a book of your own. That's how this book came to life. As a matter of fact, I wrote this paragraph while waiting for my significant other.

DISCLAIMER:

Although events and people may be familiar, the words in this book are not meant to specifically single out any one person or situation (except where I intentionally try to make it clear it's you I'm referencing). If you happen to see yourself in these pages, it is merely coincidental.

Or is it?

Stage One - Initiation

You typically wouldn't think leaving an event requires much thought or effort. To some couples, they would look at each other and say, "You ready", "Sure", "OK, let's go."

Sounds simple. But for a lot of couples, it's like getting your car from point A to point B. The first major step in that process is to put the key in the ignition.

However, like moving from point A to point B in your car, there are several other tasks required to make that happen.

There is a lead up to the commencement of leaving. Upon arrival, the exit plan starts taking shape. In the Leaver's head, there is a countdown like the countdown of the lift-off of any rocket:

10: 5000 words start getting used up
9: Avoid the people who trap you in lengthy conversations
8: Consume food
7: Consume drink
6: 2500 words used up
5: Consume more food

4:   Consume more drink
3:   Oh, look at the time
2:   The shakes (much like delirium tremens)
1:   IGNITION!

If you understand anything about personality profiles and how people are wired, you would understand that once the Leaver gets it into their head it's time to go, there really isn't much you can do to change their mind.

In the same manner, when the Stayer has it in their mind there is too much fun yet to be had, there is no way of convincing them it's time to leave.

I'm reminded of the Christmas song "Baby, It's Cold Outside" by Frank Loesser. You've probably heard it a hundred times on the radio and in movies.

In the song the woman is expressing her desire to leave, but the man is asking her to stay. She wants to go but he wants her to stay. For most couples, this is the same kind of unspoken banter that goes on inside their heads when one wants to leave and the other stay.

And, if the Stayer knows anything about personality profiles, they would spend the evening avoiding the eventual Early-Leaving tendencies of their mate by never being in the same space at the same time. That's why you often hear questions like:

"Did you see my wife?"

Or

"Did you see my husband?"

In the Initiation Stage, one part of the couple needs to put the key in the ignition to start the process. Again, simple. But when one part of the pair isn't in the car, doesn't have their coat on, still deciding on shoes or a cornucopia of other tasks to be accomplished before they are ready to leave, the task of leaving is impossible.

Again, early on, as I was developing my thoughts around the stages of leaving and in the introduction, I wanted to say the man would typically initiate this stage, but since I've learned Leavers and Stayers are gender-neutral, I can't say with confidence this is true across the board. However, I can tell you from my experience and my group of friends, it is the man, whom I fondly refer to as the "Pack Mule" or "PM" who is most interested in leaving.

I call him the Pack Mule because he is usually the person standing around holding the empty casserole dish, coats, purses and anything else that needs to go home, including the Tupperware you left at this house from the last party.

Some guys who may be more corporate minded may look at the PM role as a Project Managing role because it requires setting up meetings, negotiating positions, charts, graphs and trending past experiences to get this process of leaving underway. But for the most part, the PM usually only ends up getting it on the calendar because this will most likely be an event which happens in the future anyway. Women are more accurate when they correctly look at the man as a Pack Mule because they need somebody to carry the accoutrements of the event to the car.

Another way to look at the leaving process through the "Leaver's" eyes would be like that of the Sherpa who would guide a team of climbers from base camp to the top of Mt. Everest.

The Sherpa's job is to:

❖ prepare the route
❖ fix ropes in place
❖ carrying necessary items up the mountain

To the Leaving Sherpa, their task is difficult. They must pry their partner away from the grips of fun. This is not a task for the faint of heart. If they adopt the Sherpa stance, they must keep in mind as well, one third of the people who have died climbing Everest have been Sherpas.

The task at hand:

❖ Track down your partner
❖ Clearly communicate it is your desire to leave

❖ Maintain eye contact through the entire discourse
❖ Listen to the lie that says "Sure, I'll be right there"
❖ Reiterate your desire to leave

The Leaver must be certain to not completely use up their entire 5,000-word capacity for the day. Having done so may make communicating their desire to leave more difficult than it should be. It's quite possible when miscommunication happens at this stage it is because the Leaver made the fatal mistake of using up all their good, clear words of communication, making it difficult to get their point across in what could be a loud environment.

To the amateur Leaver, their legs will feel like lead when they start. Panic sets in because they don't yet know this isn't a sprint, but a marathon. The amateur leaver will burn themselves out quickly by trying to sprint out of the gate.

But there has got to be a starting point. I liken the Initiation Stage to one of my least favorite inventions of engineering "brilliance", the roundabout (or a big circle impeding the flow of traffic). This particular invention makes no sense to me. However, I'm sure if I were properly educated on the nuances of this death trap, this human hamster wheel, I may warm up to the idea.

Getting on and off the roundabout takes patience and a little bit of luck. It's a matter of timing, distance and accuracy. If you get on or off too quickly or get on or off too slowly, you're putting your life into your own hands.

You become subject to the yielding and merging of those who are participating in what should be a well-choreographed event. You shouldn't assume that they are paying attention. Much like the Stayer who is not watching for signs, symbols, eye contact or social queues throughout the event at hand, you need to find a way to engage them in the process in order to keep somebody from getting hurt.

I would recommend to the Leaver, if they would like to perfect the leaving process, they need to spend some time practicing on the roundabout. They need to get on and off again and again and again until they learn the nuances of the ebb and flow of those merging and yielding.

WHAT THE EXPERTS SAY

I thought I'd first start with one of world's foremost authorities on how to do things. The "Dummies Guide" people.

From <u>Dummies.com</u>, (Polite Ways For Introverts To Leave a Party Early), they seem to suggest that some of your options would be to lie.

"

- Look like you're really having a great time — not like you're relieved to escape. Say, "I'm so sorry I have to leave early. This is such a wonderful party!"

- Have an iron-clad excuse. For example, say, "I wish I could stay, but the babysitter could only stay until nine tonight."

- Arrange ahead of time for a family member to call you some time during the party with a pseudo-emergency. (Sometimes white lies are okay.)

- Tell your hosts when you accept an invitation that you'll need to leave early due to a prior commitment. That way, they won't be surprised when you slip out ahead of schedule.

- Thank your hosts before you leave. Don't just sneak away while they're occupied with other guests."

If you're going to go the "Lie" route, may I suggest a few myself:

- Oh my, I think my spleen just ruptured

- I think I left the iron on

Or my all-time favorite

- Oh, I forgot I needed to clean the lint out of the dryer.

STAGE ONE JOURNAL

STAGE ONE JOURNAL

STAGE ONE JOURNAL

STAGE ONE JOURNAL

Stage Two - Déjà Vu

I once read an article about a man in England who had reoccurring cycles of Déjà vu. Certainly not to make light of his condition because it was traumatizing for him, but it brings new light to the Yogi Berra coined phrase, "It's like Déjà vu all over again".

In the Déjà vu Stage, you find yourself reliving Stage One.

"It's like Stage One all over again".

In this stage, you loop through the same conversation with your partner where you find yourself saying things like, "you said five minutes ago you were ready".

It's sort of childish of me to glom onto the phrase, "You said". As a parent, we sometimes make the amateur parenting mistake by placing a thought into our children's still forming brains that sometime in the near future we will be doing something, anything, fill in the blank.

By placing a thought into their heads, we leave zero room for flexibility in the event something else comes up which requires us to change our plans.

Then comes the task of telling your children plans have changed. Which is promptly followed by hands hanging down by their sides' while slightly bouncing with a whining, whimpering voice that says,

"YOU SAID!"

There's no getting away from it. At that moment, you're stuck. They are correct. You did say. You said that you were going to do event A at this moment and darn it they're going make certain you fully understood the nature of the social contract into which you entered with them.

A true professional parent will navigate the waters of non-committal with ease. Their children will never know when or where they will be at any given time. At any moment, they will be swept up in the vortex of leaving. They won't know what hit them. One moment, they're coloring with chalk on the driveway and the next moment they're standing in line at Space Mountain in Disney World.

Much like that child, the Leaver will cling to any word, phrase, jot or tittle which leads them to believe you're leaning in the leaving direction. You must choose your words wisely at all times as a parent and more so as a Stayer.

The Stayer needs to learn never to commit to leaving even if they think they may want to leave.

You never know what fun will be had as a result of the next random eye contact or what fun kind of nick knacks may catch your eye as you walk past the fireplace.

You, the Stayer, can speak in vague terms or lawyer speak which sort of but not really sounds like you are committing to the act of leaving. I would never suggest you lie. I'm only suggesting you understand the nature of the Leaver and their rigid desire to GO.

You can use Latin terms such as "Ab initio" which means, "from the start of something". So you can say something like, "Ab intio I'll be contemplating an effort to vacate, but it will only be a bifurcated effort at most. And hence forth I will abscond before you at the appropriate time."

My heart cries out for the innocent people who get caught up in these stages by divine appointment. They are collateral damage. I say divine appointment because, for instance, "G" was born into our household a Leaver. G, like many innocent children, was born to a Stayer. This is cruel irony. The Lord knew G needed to be part of this family merry-go-round state of eventually leaving. G, being schedule minded, over the years endured the waiting. I've encouraged him to pick up some medical books and study in hopes by the time we leave, he will have gotten to his PHD (Please…. Hold… Door…) He's now thinking of starting his own support group called ACS (Adult Children of Stayers).

G is not alone in our friend circle. I see the orphans of Stayers (D and A) standing around, holding the keys, pie dishes, coats, etc. Some have taken to smoking. Hanging out on the streets or warming the car up, hoping they don't run out of gas this time. Again. PLEASE HELP ME is written on their faces. Like a scene out of Oliver Twist where he asks for "Another Please". Picture these children in a forlorn English accent asking, "May I go home Please".

The Déjà vu stage could possibly be a never-ending stage, reminiscent of the movie "Groundhog Day" minus the part where you can learn how to become a piano virtuoso or save the same person over and over and over again. At least at the end of the movie, the man gets the woman. The only thing you get at the end of this stage is Stage Three.

WHAT THE EXPERTS SAY

Deja Vu as describe by Judith Orloff M.D. "is a common intuitive experience that has happened to many of us. The expression is derived from the French, meaning "already seen." When it occurs, it seems to spark our <u>memory</u> of a place we have already been, a person we have already seen, or an act we have already done. It is a signal to pay special attention to what is taking place, perhaps to receive a specific lesson in a certain area or complete what is not yet finished."

(<u>https://www.psychologytoday.com/blog/emotion</u>
<u>al-freedom/201004/the-meaning-deja-vu</u>)

I would add emphasis to the author's words and state that for the Leaver, the process of leaving is "NOT YET FINISHED". This stage is yet another reminder that YOU are not finished.

STAGE TWO JOURNAL

STAGE TWO JOURNAL

STAGE TWO JOURNAL

STAGE TWO JOURNAL

STAGE TWO JOURNAL

Stage Three – A.D.D

Not to be confused with Attention Deficit Disorder. Although some may find some similarities. The acronym for this stage stands for "Anti-Destination Disorder". Another version of this acronym which we can associate with this stage is ADHD which stands for "Anti-Destination Home-averse Disorder"

Although I specifically call out the A.D.D attributes in this stage, these characteristics are prevalent through all stages and can present themselves at any given moment.

My wife Jacqueline, whom I will refer to as "J" from this point forward, is an artist on many levels. One level of her artistry is as a hair stylist.

J had asked me to install a storm/screen door on the entrance of her salon (which is attached to our house). You need to understand, I am an IT guy. In my job, I try to find the most logical, efficient ways to do things. With that in mind, I approached the task of installing the door with my IT mindset:

❖ I verified all parts were present

* ❖ I read through the instructions (Wrestled for 15 minutes with the parts of instructions which seemed incorrect)
* ❖ I reread the instructions
* ❖ I got all my tools ready
* ❖ Started the task

I don't know if you've ever tried to install a door of any kind by yourself. I quickly found out this was not a one-person job. It was clear I needed assistance.

As I was holding the door in position, I also needed to install at least two screws to hold the door in position in order to complete the install by myself.

As I was holding the heavy door in place while also trying to keep it level, I called out to J to tell her I was ready for her assistance.

At that moment, I had an immediate need. The need was to get two screws in this door before I dropped it or before it was no longer level.

I don't quite know the route J took from the kitchen to the door of her salon, but it seemed to be taking quite some time. I called out again as she was already heading in my direction. I was losing my grip (literally and figuratively) as she appeared around the corner of the porch. Relief was seconds away. Just as she was about five steps away from me I heard the dreadful words,
"Oh look, Flowers!"

In my head, the only twenty syllable word that could come to me at the time was,

"NOOOOOOOOOOOOOOOOO!"

For some of us, it is not difficult to stay on task. For others, not so much. Some are laser focused and are determined to get through steps A-Z in the most efficient and timely manner as possible. Others can get from A-Z, but seem to take many detours along the way.

As the Leaver is focused on, well, leaving, they need to be mindful of the triggers which will sidetrack the Stayer. Know your subject. The looks and sounds of the distracted Stayer go something like this:

- "Oh my goodness, is that not the cutest baby ever. He's so chunky. I could just nibble on his toes" (Babies will sidetrack you in an instant)
- "I love those shoes; from where did you get them"
- "Ohhh, What perfume is that? It smells so woodsy"
- "Hiiiiiiiii" (that's a very long excited, high-pitched "Hi")
- "Oh, I forgot my purse" (Translations: "Oh, I forgot I really didn't want to leave"
- "I LOVE this song"
- "Heeeey Macarena"
- "Everybody dance now. Dun dun dun"

Any one of those distractions are a clear, direct path back to Stage One. Do not pass Go, do not collect $200.

The Leaver needs to stay close to the Stayer. The Leaver needs to run interference to any perceived distraction between you, the Stayer and the door. Heck, between you and home. You need to anticipate everybody and everything's next move.

It's like the Tri-Dimensional Chess set (Franklin Mint Set for $440 on Amazon.com) as seen in a Star Trek episode. Star Trek the original, not The Next Generation (my favorite).

Keep in mind, once you've successfully navigated Stage Three, you cannot let your guard down. Thus, the reason for the Déjà vu Stage (Stage Two).

Here is a real-life example of how the A.D.D. Stage plays out. My wife got the following text from our friend Susan on Sunday morning.

Susan:
"What stage of leaving is it when your husband calls at 11:43am and says he's leaving church. You live 17 minutes from said church. And 50 minutes later he still isn't home."

Susan suggested we create a new stage called:

Susan:

"I don't think about the fact my wife is a person who tends to be aware of time and might worry that I'm dead on the side of the road DISORDER Stage"

Clearly, this fits into the A.D.D. Stage. I thought it would be interesting to get Jeff's side of the story. Jeff provided the following diagram which depicts the route he followed once he communicated he was on his way home.

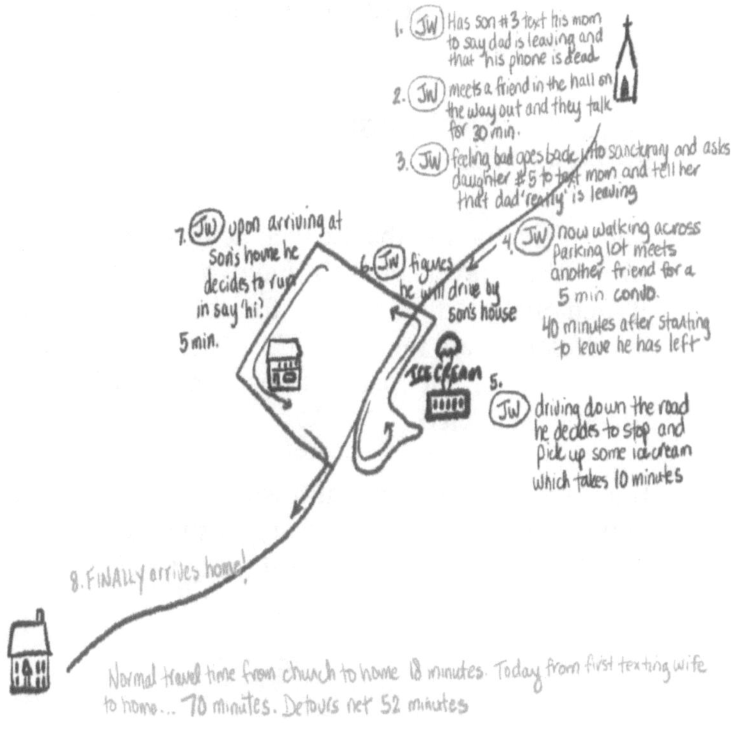

WHAT THE EXPERTS SAY

In her "addditudemag.com " article, Beth Main talks about "Why It's Hard to Stay on Task". She states:

"For adults with ADHD, keeping a mental to-do list just doesn't work. It takes up brain bandwidth you could be using for other things. You forget stuff and then remember while you're in the middle of doing something else. You jump up to do it, and never go back to the original thing. Your natural tendency for impulsivity takes over, and that can be stressful. **Detailed planning for how to stay on task is the answer.**"

(https://www.additudemag.com/slideshows/how-to-stay-on-task/)

The difficulty for the Leaver at this time comes when the Stayer doesn't have a detailed plan. Which makes it important for the Leaver to be mindful that all the Leaver's plans in the world will not alter the path of the Stayer once they become distracted.

It's your job to remove all distraction between the Stayer and home. If you are unsuccessful, your only hope is for Role Reversal (Stage 4).

STAGE THREE JOURNAL

STAGE THREE JOURNAL

STAGE THREE JOURNAL

STAGE THREE JOURNAL

Stage Four – Role Reversal

Roles are pretty well defined in every relationship. We are all pretty much hardwired to be who we are. On rare occasions, we find ourselves stepping outside of who we are.

Recently I found myself in deep conversation with a man after church. This, in and of itself was a Role Reversal for me because I perceive myself to typically not be that talkative after church. (Or so I thought. More to come on this)

As I was talking with this man, I was taken off guard when my PINK HAIRED daughter Z approached me to tell me, "Dad, Mom is ready to go".

I'm sure you've heard the sound effect which sounds like a vinyl record being stopped on a turntable as the needle runs through the grooves. (Note: You millennial's will just have to Google that one). That's the sound that went through my head at that very moment. It's like, "Wait, What!". I had to process that last sentence in my head for a moment. This was a needle across the record moment for me. It was unusual to be in the position where I wasn't pacing waiting to leave. I was now holding up progress. Or so I thought.

"Dad, Mom is ready to go".

There is no greater example of a Role Reversal I can use to make my point than that one perplexing statement.

It would be like my friend Jeff immediately picking up and leaving at the end of an event. Susan, his wife, would be there scratching her head wondering what just happened. I'm sure there would be some level of concern there may be something wrong with Jeff.

I know many of you may not know J or Jeff, but you do have a version of them in your life and could relate if the above scenarios occurred with them.

How interesting it is for the typical Stayer to give you that look which communicates, "come on, I've been waiting for you". It's hard not to be indignant at that moment. You find yourself looking over your shoulder and all around to see if anybody else saw what just happened. It's as if you were the first person to ever see a unicorn.

It takes everything in you to not point out this is the very feeling you experience at the end of every event. It's hard not to do a victory lap, a dance of joy or even drag your feet a bit. But for the most part, you can't help yourself. By nature, you are a

Leaver. And given the opportunity, you're going to leave.

On a side note, sometimes the Leaver gets caught off guard thinking they have a little more time because the "Stayers gunna stay". Suddenly, they find themselves being the last one out the door, thus looking like the bottleneck to the leaving process.

You also need to remember, the Stayer, by nature, is hardwired to stay. At any moment, there may be an Anti-Destination Disorder trigger. So, suck it up, keep your mouth shut, get in the car and Go for the love of Pete.

Years ago, I was introduced to Tae Kwon Do. Translated – "the way of the foot and fist". In my training, we were taught what is called "One Step Sparring". In it's simplest form, we were taught to instantly react to a certain situation with a kick, a punch or block without thinking. We practiced it repeatedly throughout the years so without thinking we could, through instinct, act.

 If a Leaver finds themselves in this position, they need to break out their best Bruce Lee and spring into action. If not, they'll never know what just hit them. If they don't, it will look something like a jumping 360 degree back hook kick that sounds something like this.

"Never mind, Mom is talking to Susan"

In my daytime profession, I like to improve processes by taking away inefficiencies. Workflow improvements are the results of removing those inefficiencies.

I also try to make practical adjustments in my life outside of work to streamline repeatable processes. For instance, I've perfected the order of the way I cleanse myself in the shower. I've shaved off minutes over the years.

What I've found is, if I do things out of order, I forget to do other things, thinking that the prerequisite has already been done. Recently, in the shower I had done something out of order. When I got to work that day I realized I forgot to shave. When I thought back to my time in the shower, I was able to pinpoint the break in process. I've noted it and am certain I won't do that again.

On one occasion in the role reversal stage, my friend Jeff (AKA Jeff) was sitting in his car and said he was ready to go and Susan, his wife, said, "I can't believe you're in the car and I'm still talking". Susan stood up, paused and said, "I've never heard that statement from Jeff in thirty-seven years of marriage".

Wait, there is more. Because they were in role reversal and leaving out of sequence, they almost left without their children. True Story!

WHAT THE EXPERTS SAY

"Role reversal is one of the psychodrama techniques that demonstrate a protagonist's intrapersonal conflicts deeply and explicitly on the stage.[1] This technique is perhaps the single most important and effective technique in psychodrama. In the form of psychodrama, the protagonist is invited to move out of their own position or role into the significant other's position and enact that role. Therefore, the auxiliary ego can observe and learn how to play the role. For example, in a parent-child's session, a protagonist who is the child reverses role with one of his or her parents. This technique not only helps the protagonist get more insight of a specific role but also helps the director, the auxiliary egos, and the audience learn more about that specific role."

(https://en.wikipedia.org/wiki/Role_reversal)

STAGE FOUR JOURNAL

STAGE FOUR JOURNAL

STAGE FOUR JOURNAL

STAGE FOUR JOURNAL

STAGE FOUR JOURNAL

Stage Five - Bait & Switch

As you thumb through the advertisement section of any newspaper or magazine, you may be struck by a deal which seems too good to be true. But there it is, in writing, staring you right in the face.

You need to check this out for yourself because, well, it's too good to be true. You quickly find your way to the purveyor of this wonderful deal only to find they are out of stock and willing to sell you an even better product at a much higher price. You, my friend, have just experienced Bait and Switch.

The Bait and Switch stage occurs when the Leaver is excited and thinks they are on their way out the door. When suddenly, BAM! They are at Stage One all over again.

Typically, a Bait and Switch like the above example is done with nefarious intentions. Although the Leaver feels like they've been dealt a bait and switch hand, it really has nothing to do with the Stayer. Nor did the Stayer have nefarious intentions.

The Bait and Switch happens in the Leaver's head. This is a result of an expectation created in the

Leaver's head at some point throughout the duration of the event at hand.

For instance, if the Stayer grabs a set of keys or a purse, the Leaver automatically has a Pavlovian response, thus implanting an image of leaving in their head.

Much like the "You Said" scenario discussed in the Déjà vu Stage (Stage Two), the Stayer inadvertently planted a seed which immediately takes root and needs no watering to grow.

For me, Bait and Switch takes many forms. For instance, as an introvert, my batteries get charged from alone time. Some solitude. I can think of many times throughout my marriage when coming home from a long, stressful day of work looking forward to some time to unwind, only to come home to a spontaneous gathering of people at my house.

The thoughts of putting my feet up and relaxing for a bit have been replaced with ten kids running around with air soft rifles and pistols trying not to shoot each other's eyes out while trying to keep the house from being burned down because, simultaneously children are being introduced to the fine art of flame throwing Fondue.

Of course, I exaggerate, but that's how things reverberate in the introvert's head. Although You are not the one trying to leave the event because the event found it's way to you, there are now seven new stages unexpectedly foisted upon your introverted self.

In all stages, there is collateral damage. One of the definitions of Collateral Damage is "any damage incidental to an activity". Some would call it consequences.

There are both positive and negative consequences to everything we do. For the most part those consequences go unnoticed. For instance, five seconds of me checking a text on my phone before leaving for the gym in the morning can mean I get stuck behind a school bus or even worse, I would hit that one red light which seemingly takes hours to turn green. I end up trying to roll back and forth over the light's pressure plate to get it to acknowledge my existence, in the same way you would like to garner attention of the person behind the counter at the DMV.

When I get stuck at long lights, I get sucked into the trap of believing I now have all the time in the world to check some work email. By doing so, I miss the fact that the light has turned green and now I become the guy holding up everyone else.

When I'm not paying attention and get a late start out of the gate, I feel mostly sorry for the guy who didn't make the green light because of my two second delay. And I'm thankful I never get to enjoy the sign language being hurled in my direction or the niceties being spoken about me by the guy in the car now stuck at the red light is "Collateral Damage".

I've recently coined a new phrase, "The Thomas Effect". You can search for this in all the physics literature you want, but you won't find it there.

The Thomas Effect goes something like this. (True story by the way). While leaving a friend's house for a date with J (to our favorite sushi place where I will predictably get a chicken tempura roll because it doesn't have salmonella as part of its ingredients), another friend, Thomas pulled up in the driveway in his BRAND SPANKING NEW car, blocking our car from leaving. Of course, J was excited to see Thomas and his new car. But she was now torn because she knew I was most interested in getting to our destination on time.

She was now entering the A.D.D Stage while I was feeling the effects of entering the Bait and Switch Stage. J, in an attempt at Role Reversal, threw herself on the sword for the team and rushed Thomas through his visit so we could leave before all of the very loud college students showed up at our sushi restaurant.

During the excitement, Thomas, in his efforts to clear the way so my selfish needs would be met, backed his BRAND SPANKING NEW car into a tree!

Thomas' car now became Collateral Damage, but I got my chicken tempura roll and no salmonella. (Thank you for your grace Thomas.)

WHAT THE EXPERTS SAY

In his article, Rob Bignell says, "Use bait-and-switch device carefully in stories", the "time-honored way to make your plot more interesting is to employ a bait-and-switch device."

This occurs when the author guides and encourages readers to invest their attention in some suspenseful situation but then is substitute for a payoff that has little to do with what occurred before. Getting readers to invest their attention is the bait; substituting a payoff is the switch."

(https://inventingrealityeditingservice.typepad.com/inventing_reality_editing/2013/04/use-bait-and-switch-device-carefully-in-stories.html)

STAGE FIVE JOURNAL

STAGE FIVE JOURNAL

STAGE FIVE JOURNAL

STAGE FIVE JOURNAL

Stage Six - The Farewell Tour

If you are familiar with the band Kiss, you know that they go all out with their makeup for their concerts. Some may not know that the band had a season where they performed without makeup. At a point they broke up and the came together for a "Reunion Tour" in 1996. They then planned their farewell tour for 2000. This was intended to be their last tour.

Like any great band, the farewell tour is meant to give their fans one last performance before they hang it up. Kiss was no different. At that time, they performed their last farewell show in South Carolina.

For the Leaver, the farewell tour begins when they stick out their chest and pull their shoulders back as they strut by their stranded friends who are sitting there all slack-jawed wondering when their fortunes will change. They walk in a manner that says "Yes, I'm in the go-mode. Look at you poor, pathetic saps just sitting there, sipping away on your 100th beer with some German name as the label slowly slips down the curve of the bottle because the level of condensation between a once cold bottle has now mixed with the warm sweat on the palms of your hands. "Look at me go!". At this point it's all about the competition.

This is the Leaver's victory march. It's a celebration of the end of an era. But this could quickly turn into a death march.

While the Stayer rejoices in laughter and conversation with EVERY SINGLE PERSON (Leaver's emphasis) who remains, leaving becomes as difficult as prying the plastic off a new CD case you recently purchased. For those of you under a certain age, I'm sure that CD reference was lost on you. If you didn't get that reference, try wrapping your head around the concept of an 8-Track tape. Go ahead, Google that.

One would think there is light at the end of the tunnel for the Leaver. For the Leaver, it's important not to gloat too much. Any lingering is to your detriment. The professional Stayer will make their rounds on the way out the door. For the most part, the "Goodbyes" happen on the path on the way to the door. Of course, the host of any event should be the last person on your Goodbye list. It becomes tricky when the host is stationed at the farthest point from the door. The professional Leaver will try to time their exit when the host is closest to the door.

Now, depending on the event and the guests, the sequence of Goodbye have varying levels of importance. If, for instance, you are at a wedding where you only know the bride or groom and nobody else, extricating yourself is simpler than a wedding of a family member or a member of your friend group.

At an event where your parents, aunts, uncles and cousins are present, you need to carefully pick the order of goodbyes in order to not offend the most sensitive of the group. If you find yourself at odds with any of those members, you may want to save them for last. This will give them a sense of importance and gain you some valuable points which can be used when you make an unfortunate misstep in the future.

There may be that arch nemesis who is never pleased with anything you do. You'll probably want to say goodbye to them first in order to hack them off just a little bit more. Why not, you'll never improve your standing in their eyes no matter what you do anyway.

It's during this stage when the S.E.E (Strategic Exit Eating) happens. At this time, you find yourself making one more pass of the food table. If you're anything like me, you've already determined which morsel of food you want to cram down your gullet as you walk out the door. For me, it would be any version of chocolate cake. And creamy buffalo chicken dip, peanut m&m's. Or pie. Cookies are ideal because you can fit them in your pocket. Chips. Definitely chips. Oh, chips and buffalo dip. A trifecta would be to end with Chips, chocolate and peanut butter.

As you can tell, I have an issue with food. (Don't judge me).

For the Stayer, the Farewell Tour is different. For them it is a somber moment. The dreaded FOMO (Fear Of Missing Out) sickness gnaws at their inmost being.

But there is no doubt, although sad, there is plenty of party yet to be had as the Leaver weaves their way through the labyrinth of people and other distractions on their way to the exit.

If the Stayer properly times their exit, they can actually be the last person out the door, completely eliminating their sadness and FOMO feelings while retaining the sense that they orchestrated the whole thing while the Leaver is then left standing there holding their warm beer with no label, having watched all their buddies go through their Farewell Tour.

By the way, as of this writing, eighteen years later, Kiss has announced its "End of the Road Farewell Tour". So, you can see, a farewell tour doesn't always mean what you think it means. For the Stayer, they can have as many farewell tours as they like. And you, the Leaver, must endure the emotional suffering and head back to Stage 5, the "Bait and Switch" stage.

WHAT THE EXPERTS SAY

From PsychologyToday.com:

(https://www.psychologytoday.com/blog/the-introverts-corner/201008/there-must-be-50-ways-leave-party)

"Of course, if you go to a party with an extrovert, prying that person out early is difficult, and unfair. That's why you should bring your own wheels (or cab fare) whenever possible. You probably won't break your friend's heart by leaving on your own. *By the time you leave, your extrovert friend will have found a new and shiny friend,* wrote Kelly Parkinson.

So, don't worry about it. Slip out the back, or put on a big smile and parade out, waving and air kissing. Just remember that if you allow yourself to leave parties when you're ready, you're more likely to enjoy them while you're there."

STAGE SIX JOURNAL

STAGE SIX JOURNAL

STAGE SIX JOURNAL

STAGE SIX JOURNAL

Stage Seven - Ignition

Although Stage Seven starts when the key is turned to the on position in the ignition of your vehicle, this doesn't necessarily mean the seven stages are complete.

Any leaving amateur could quickly be pulled back into any one of the earlier stages. It could have taken as little as a few minutes or as much as an hour or more to reach this stage. Caution must be taken at such a critical time that you don't lose control of stage Seven.

If, for some reason, you make a fatal error, you may find yourself lying in the corner of the room in a fetal position sucking your thumb, wondering what went wrong. You'll feel much like the guy outlined in chalk behind the police barrier.

Stage Seven is exciting and quite an achievement for both the Stayer and the Leaver. The Stayer endured to this point, causing the Leaver to navigate their way through the six previous stages. It's quite possible the Leaver made their way through some of the stages multiple times. And the Leaver surpassed even their own expectation in getting to this point. High five's all around, but not just yet. Don't get cocky.

One of my favorite things to do is watch professional football games (not soccer, I'd rather poke a stick in my ear hole than watch that). Prior to meeting my wife, I had put an ISO (In Search Of) ad in our local newspaper. For those of you who don't know what that is, it was a very primitive version of MATCH.COM.

ISO ads were used to find a date based on certain criteria. One particular criterion of mine was a woman who loved football. I had other criteria such as needing to love the Lord, be tall and have red hair. (Don't judge me)

Of course, when I met my wife, because she was tall and a red head, the need for her to love football quickly went out the window. The only part of football which pertains to J is she lives on football time, particularly the two-minute warning. If you are unfamiliar with the last two minutes of a football game, this period of time can stretch out to fifteen minutes or more.

I give the above context because this stage, unlike most of the earlier stages, feels the most like the last two minutes of a football game.

Sometimes, when a football game comes down to the wire and the team is behind, the coach has two options. The first option is to hand the ball off or pass it, then lateral the ball to another player and then another player and then another player in the hopes somebody misses a tackle, freeing up the runner to run the rest of the way for a touchdown. (by the way, I don't recall ever seeing that work)

The second, and more successful option is the Hail Mary pass. This last-ditch effort play is designed to have all of the players eligible to catch a ball run to the end zone while the quarterback throws the ball as high as he possibly can and as far as he possibly can in the hopes the heavens will open up and a miracle will come upon them by having one of his teammates finally end up with the ball. If all of a sudden you see crowds of people surrounding your significant other, you know they are going for the Hail Mary of staying. You need to put in your best defense at this moment, because you know the game is on the line and the crowd is watching. (That would be your buddies with the German beers)

If you've gotten to this stage and the Stayer of the group is hanging on for dear life, you have your own Hail Mary Option at your disposal. This option comes with a secret code word which I can only share with you in the confines of this book. In the wrong hands this code word could be used for malicious reasons. But I'm taking a chance by sharing this with you. In the event you can't successfully pull off Stage Seven and you must pull out your Hail Mary Option. Also known as the Nuclear Option. You only need to call out

"UBER" (Unconventional Bifurcated Exit Request). Once you've used the UBER code word, you've instantly created a clear and direct path to home.

By now, you've exhausted the stages. Your words have probably run out two hours ago, but still have enough words left to say, "thank you for inviting us. We had a lovely time. We must do this again sometime"

With mock sadness you feign somberness as you walk out the door. Your Staying counterpart's look of sadness is that of genuine grief. Any good host will have a grief counselor stationed at every exit point.

WHAT THE EXPERTS SAY

From <u>http://www.slate.com/blogs/entertaining/20</u>
<u>13/09/13/slate_s_rules_for_entertaining_when_to_</u>
<u>leave_a_party_at_the_end_of_the_night.html</u>

<u>Slate.Com</u> addresses the Beloved Stayer, the one everybody seems to revere. That is unless of course you are the host.

J. Bryan Lowder in this article seems to suggest the host eventually comes to an understanding of the Leaver's plight when Lowder suggests the host finally "tell people after a dinner party to get the 'bleep' out if they won't leave".

Lowder is not addressing the traditional Stayer who knows the proper boundaries when it comes to leaving. Lowder is addressing the Ultra-Stayer. The people who awkwardly stay even while the hosts eyes are rolling in the backs of their collective heads trying to stay awake. I guess the host may eventually have to bring out the big boy words and eventually tell the Ultra-Stayer to "Get the 'bleep' out of our house".

DON'T BE THAT PERSON!
Of course, there is the occasional couple which makes up the "Perfect Storm". They would be the couple made up of two Leavers. I immediately knew the one couple I met recently were the Perfect Storm when it took them no less than twenty

minutes to pick their cocktails off the menu at the restaurant. I knew then we weren't getting home any time soon.

STAGE SEVEN JOURNAL

STAGE SEVEN JOURNAL

STAGE SEVEN JOURNAL

STAGE SEVEN JOURNAL

Testimonials

Chris

(not to be confused with The Ghost) is a marathoner when it comes to leaving. Chris, says the following:

"I don't have 7 stages, I am a Leaver and my wife a Stayer.

We play a game, I tell her I don't want to go, she says we aren't staying cause she is tired and that we are leaving early.

I pretend to believe her and the game and frustration begins.

At some point, she will say are you ready? I always say yes (hoping and praying it will end soon), knowing that if she doesn't get up at that very moment- it's another 3+ hours. If by some chance she does get up the good-byes are at least an hour as we make our way to the exit.

I am now resolved to stay to the end or not go."

Bill
(author of this book)

Actual words spoken by J:

"I'm ready to go, but I have 10 things to do first"

Conclusion

(What I Learned About Myself)

I've had some fun over the years developing the thoughts expressed in this book. Possibly at the expense of those I love. However, those who know me, know I love them dearly and have discussed these ideas with them at length over the years and are pretty much on board with my theories.

On March 6th, 2018 I had an epiphany. Actually, it hit me right smack in the face. It would have been helpful years earlier to have gained this bit of knowledge. That knowledge is, for the Stayer, every social gathering is a party. In the bathroom, in a hallway, in the elevator, at church, they are having a party.

In the chapters above, I portray myself as somebody eager to not be in or around groups of people. I often thought I want to be like my one friend whom I'll call the Ghost because he was there one moment and gone the next as if he was never there. But in reality, I'm pointing out a flaw in my character which took me years to realize.

I often have said that if you want to be something, you need to surround yourself with people who are that same something. I have a bit of a counseling background and know a bit about personalities and personality profiles. There are several on the market like Enneagram, Myers Briggs and DISC Profile.

Over time the different profiles seem to get mixed up in my mind or I forget which designations belong to which profile type.

But not my friends, they seem to know all the profile tools. I find it odd that a lot of my friends and even my children can spout off their Enneagram wings or their Myers Briggs designation. And they wear it like a badge of honor. I wanted to be a counselor. Inadvertently, I've surrounded myself with a bunch of "Counselors".

For the purposes of this book, I needed a refresher course to bring myself up to speed on the different profiles. So now I can say I'm a Myers Briggs ISTJ or and Enneagram 5 and everyone I know, knows what that means.

For the most part, it means I'm wired like my other ISTJ friends and do not get my batteries charged in crowd settings. I get my batteries charged in solitude. Although I'm not uncomfortable in crowds, at times in my head I'm searching for the nearest exit.

I've always viewed myself as the guy who didn't speak much in crowds. For the most part, I still believe that to be true. But during a recent mid-year review at my company, it was revealed to me that I'm a talker. I know, I was just as shocked to find this out myself.

At the end of my review, when my boss Chris got to the part where he challenged me to grow, he encouraged me to be less verbose in meetings.

In my mind I had to step back for a moment. I was thinking, "wait a minute, has he mixed up my appraisal with another colleague's". I was wondering if he was talking to me at that moment. Did he really know who I was? I often thought of myself as the person who spoke the least in meetings and was shocked to find this out about myself. You could say I was dumbfounded.

Upon arriving at home that evening, I shared this heresy with my wife and son Gabriel. I was expecting a firm agreement from them both that my boss was clearly mistaken. My wife turned to my son and asked, "who speaks the most in this household". I was certain he would, without hesitation say "Mom". Without hesitation he turns and pointed to me. Instantly he was cut out of my will which will make Kaleigh, Blair and Zoë very happy.

In retrospect, they were all correct. Apparently, I'm one of those people who talks a lot. Not only do I talk a lot, I can give out the least amount of information with the maximum amount of words. For instance, I used almost an entire chapter to say, "I talk a lot". I know my good friend and fellow introvert Susan will be shocked to know that I'm a closet talker.

I've since joined a support group for this. The group is called "On and On Anon".

"Hello everybody, my name is Bill and I'm a Talk-Aholic!"

What I realize, especially with my wife, she loves people. She loves being around them. Laughing with them. Loving them. Crying with them. Agonizing with them. Worshiping and Praising with them.

Deep down inside, that is who I want to be. We were not made to be alone. We were made to live in community.

As a Leaver, I need to show grace towards the Stayer. I think deep down inside the Stayers want to be Leavers and the Leavers want to be Stayers. Who am I kidding, Stayers just want to stay.

But in the end, we all find good in each other's personalities. Sometimes the parts of the personalities of others that rub us the wrong way are the same parts that make us love them.

If we sat down and thought about it, we would much rather have the good parts of The Stayer or Leaver's personalities that is outweighed by what we sometimes think is the bad part of their personality. However, it's those parts of their personalities that also makes The Stayer or Leaver good in our eyes. To tear out even a small part of that person would make him or her different. So much so we would no longer find them attractive.

To go even deeper, I'm learning my rigid desire to get up and go is less loving than my wife who is so engrossed in the community at hand that leaving is the last thing on her mind. I covet that part of the personality of a person who is relational and just happy to be with people.

Therefore, when you see me at a party or at church, I hope to be the guy comfortably in conversation, cocking my head back in laughter as I listen to the stories, not caring what time it is or whether or not it's time to go. And If I am, I'm sure it will be written all over my face.

I know this was a quick read. Some may find it took less time to read this book than it does to extract their significant other from any given event but I thank you for having a bit of fun with me. Please look for the more serious version of this book which discusses the Seven Stages of Leaving. (Signs and Symptom of Couples in Crisis on Their Way to Divorce).

CULTURAL CONSIDERATIONS

It's important to point out we can't assume leaving would look the same across all cultures. Much like gender, you may find that not everybody with the same cultural roots will leave in the same manner. I am considering adding a cultural section to the next edition of this book.

AUTHOR's NOTE:

On the very day I was putting the final touches on this book, J was telling us all it's time to go to church. I'm not kidding when I say it took me less than three minutes to change my shoes to get ready to leave. When I said I'm ready after that three minutes, I found J in her salon giving G a haircut. And this scenario is the whole basis of my book.

READER'S THOUGHTS

READER'S THOUGHTS

READER'S THOUGHTS